my friendly neighborhood

Veterinarian

Published in the United States of America by Cherry Lake Publishing
Ann Arbor, Michigan
www.cherrylakepublishing.com

Reading Adviser: Marla Conn MS, Ed., Literacy specialist, Read-Ability, Inc.
Book Design: Jennifer Wahi
Illustrator: Jeff Bane

Photo Credits: © Monkey Business Images / Shutterstock.com, 5, 21; © Ermolaev Alexander / Shutterstock.com, 7; © Brent Reeves / Shutterstock.com, 9; © Lucky Business / Shutterstock.com, 11; © Bork / Shutterstock.com, 13; © 135pixels / Shutterstock.com, 15; © Blanscape / Shutterstock.com, 17; © XiXinXing / Shutterstock.com, 19; © romul014 / Shutterstock.com, 23; © aleksandr-mansurov-ru, 2-3, 24; Cover, 1, 6, 8, 16, Jeff Bane

Copyright ©2018 by Cherry Lake Publishing
All rights reserved. No part of this book may be reproduced or utilized in any form or by any means without written permission from the publisher.

Library of Congress Cataloging-in-Publication Data

Names: Bell, Samantha, author. | Bane, Jeff, 1957- illustrator.
Title: Veterinarian / Samantha Bell ; [illustrated by Jeff Bane].
Description: Ann Arbor, MI : Cherry Lake Publishing, [2017] | Series: My friendly neighborhood | Audience: K to grade 3.
Identifiers: LCCN 2016056588| ISBN 9781634728300 (hardcover) | ISBN 9781534100084 (pbk.) | ISBN 9781634729192 (pdf) | ISBN 9781534100978 (hosted ebook)
Subjects: LCSH: Veterinarians--Juvenile literature.
Classification: LCC SF756 .B44 2017 | DDC 636.089--dc23
LC record available at https://lccn.loc.gov/2016056588

Printed in the United States of America
Corporate Graphics

table of contents

Neighborhood Helper 4

Glossary 24

Index 24

About the author: Samantha Bell has written and illustrated over 60 books for children. She lives in South Carolina with her family and pets. She is very thankful for the helpers in her community.

About the illustrator: Jeff Bane and his two business partners own a studio along the American River in Folsom, California, home of the 1849 Gold Rush. When Jeff's not sketching or illustrating for clients, he's either swimming or kayaking in the river to relax.

neighborhood helper

Veterinarians are called vets.
They are animal doctors.

Pets get sick. The vet gives pets **medicine**. It helps pets feel better.

What is your favorite pet?

Some vets help dogs and cats.

Some vets help birds and snakes.

Some work in zoos. They help lions and monkeys.

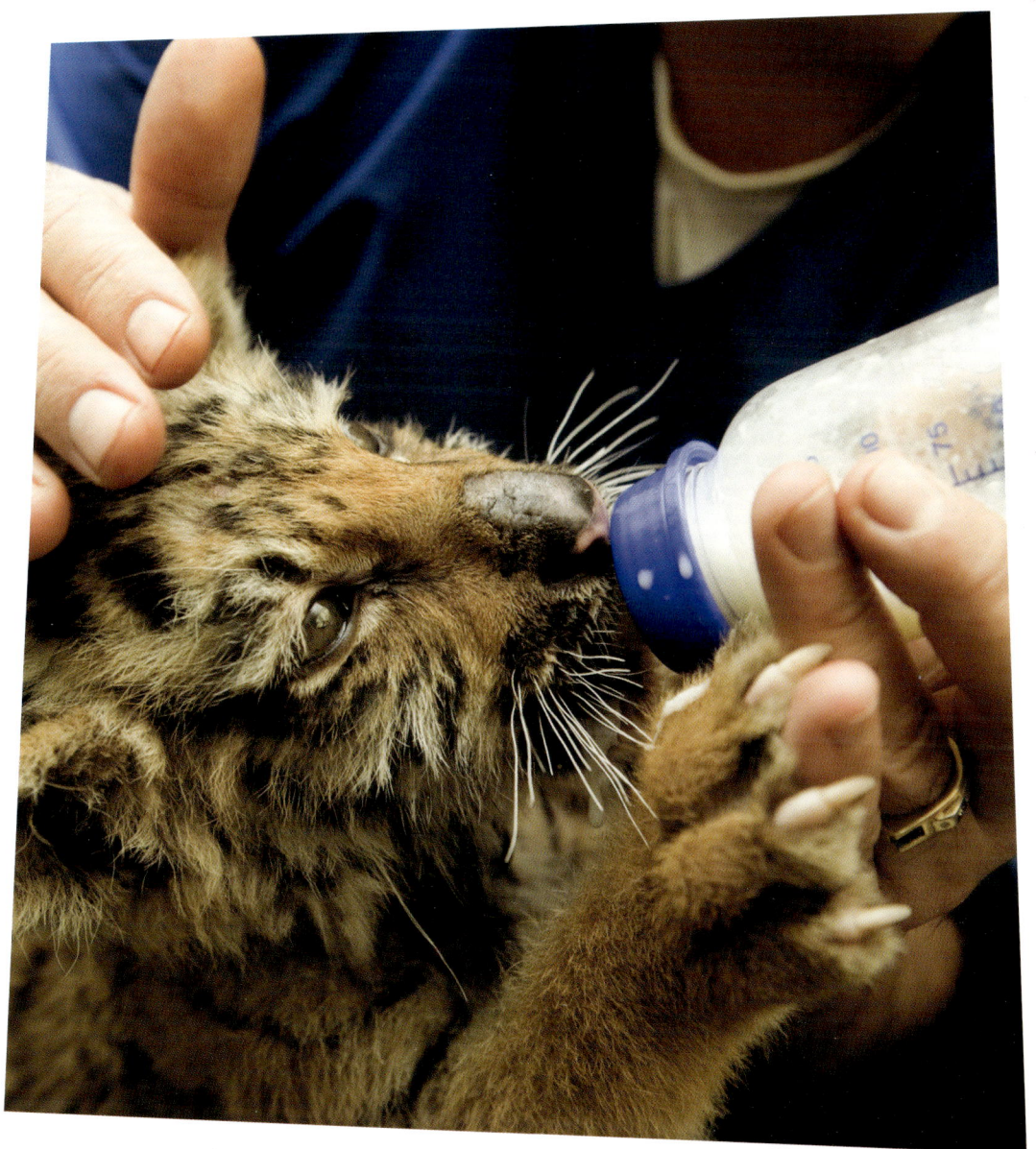

Some work on farms. They help horses and cows.

What is another farm animal?

Sometimes pets break bones.
The vet fixes the bones.

Some vets help in an **emergency**.
They take care of pets right away.

Sometimes pets must stay with the vet. The pets stay in **kennels**. The vet keeps them warm.

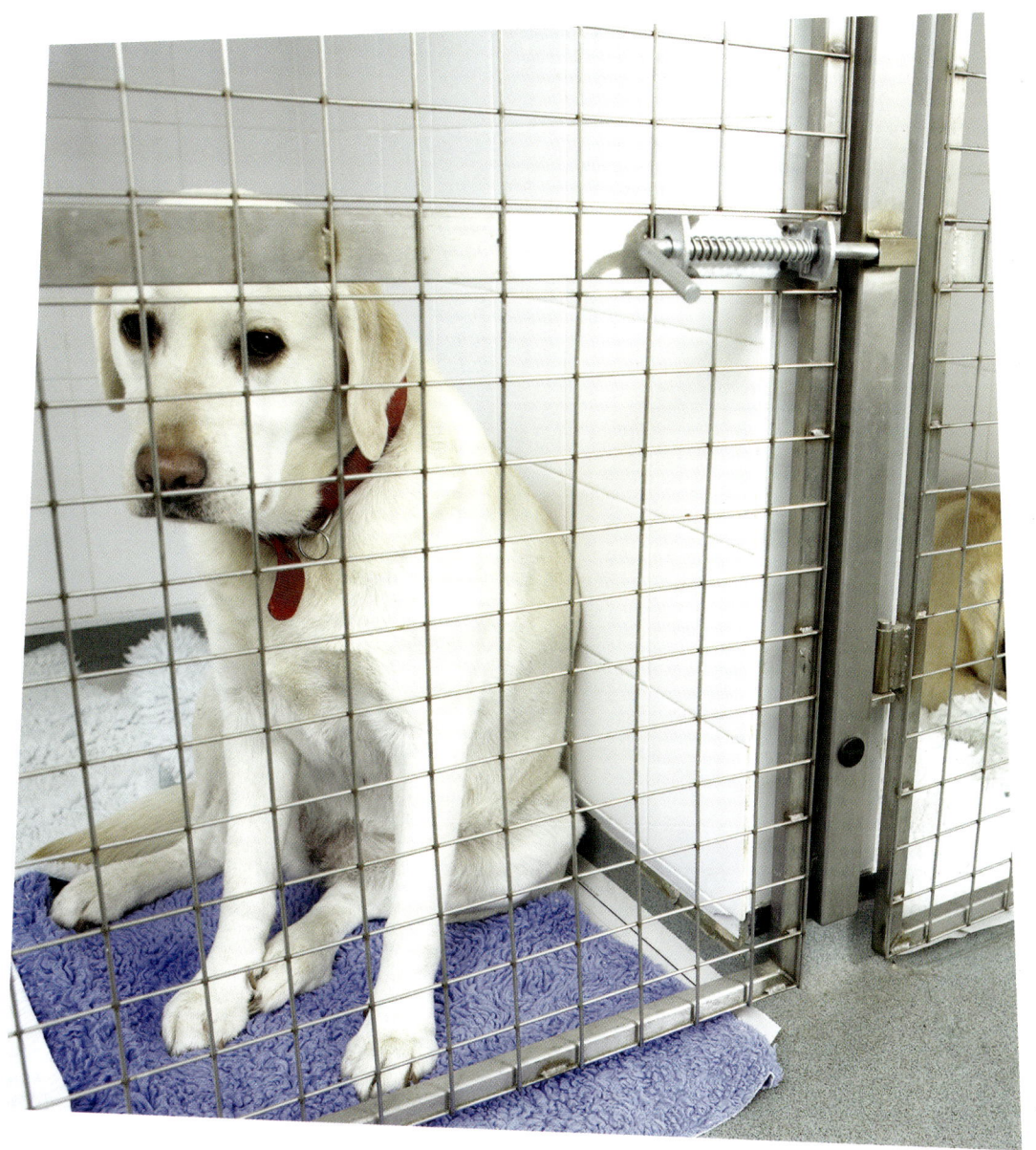

Vets know a lot about pets.
They give people **advice**.

What would you like to ask a veterinarian?

glossary & index

glossary

advice (uhd-VICE) an opinion or suggestion about what to do

emergency (ih-MUR-juhn-see) a sudden problem that requires help right away

kennels (KEN-uhlz) small shelters for dogs or cats

medicine (MED-ih-sin) helpful drugs used to treat illnesses

index

advice, 22
animal doctors, 4

emergency, 18

kennels, 20

medicine, 6

pets, 6-7, 16, 18, 20, 22